Polar Babies

Maya Myers

NATIONAL
GEOGRAPHIC

Washington, D.C.

Vocabulary Tree

Baby animals

leveret
cub
pup
calf
owlet
chick
kit

What keeps them warm and safe

fur
blubber
sun
food
feathers
parents

father   mother

arctic fox kits

Can you find the polar animal babies?

The top and bottom of Earth are called poles.

emperor penguin chicks

There is ice and snow at the poles.
Many polar babies live there.

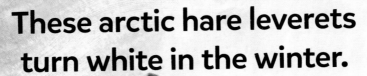

These arctic hare leverets turn white in the winter.

arctic hare leverets

arctic hares

Their white fur hides them in the
snow. This keeps them safe.

polar bear cub

Fur keeps polar animals warm.
This cub has thick fur.

To take a bath, the cub rubs its fur on the snow!

9

harp seal pup

This seal pup has a thick layer of fat called blubber.

harp seal

The blubber keeps
the pup warm.

A walrus calf snuggles with its mother.

walrus

walrus calf

The sun keeps them warm even though they sleep on ice!

13

Snowy owlets cuddle in a hollow on the ground.

snowy owlets

Their father swoops in, bringing food. Yum!

snowy owl

beluga whale

Some polar animals
live in the cold water.

beluga whale calf

A beluga calf swims
close to its mother.

An emperor penguin chick has fuzzy gray feathers.

emperor penguin chick

emperor penguins

Later, it will grow smooth feathers.
Feathers keep penguins dry.

Where is the muskox calf?

muskox calf

It is next to its mother.
Their fur coats are very cozy!

muskoxen

21

Polar babies have what they need to stay warm and safe!

arctic fox kit

Your Turn!

Can you stay warm like these polar babies?

Can you lie in the sun like a sea otter pup?

Can you sleep in a cozy cave like an arctic wolf pup?

Can you wear a thick coat like a reindeer calf?

Can you snuggle up like a stoat kit?

For Dillon, our polar explorer —M.M.

polar bear cub

Published by National Geographic Partners, LLC, Washington, DC 20036.

Copyright © 2025 National Geographic Partners, LLC

Designed by Gustavo Tello

The author and publisher gratefully acknowledge the literacy review of this book by Mariam Jean Dreher, professor emerita of reading education, University of Maryland, College Park, and content review by animal and education experts at Disney's Animals, Science and Environment.

Trade paperback ISBN: 978-1-4263-7786-0
Reinforced library binding ISBN: 978-1-4263-7787-7

Photo Credits
Cover, Keren Su/Danita Delimont; 1, Jenny E. Ross/Nature Picture Library; 2-3, Klein & Hubert/Nature Picture Library; 2-3 (polar illustrations throughout), Six Red Marbles; 4, Samuel Lima/Adobe Stock; 5, Klein & Hubert/Nature Picture Library; 6, Jim Brandenburg/Minden Pictures; 7, Jack Stephens/Alamy Stock Photo; 8, Daisy Gilardini; 9, Belovodchenko Anton/Shutterstock; 10-11, Jennifer Hayes/National Geographic Image Collection; 12, Jami Tarris/Minden Pictures; 13, Norbert Rosing/National Geographic Image Collection; 14-15, Michio Hoshino/Minden Pictures; 14 (inset), Michio Hoshino/Minden Pictures; 16-17, imageBROKER/Adobe Stock; 18, Konrad Wothe/Minden Pictures; 19, Doug Allan/Nature Picture Library; 20-21, Tsugaru Yutaka/Minden Pictures; 22, Klein & Hubert/Nature Picture Library; 23 (UP LE), Jaynes Gallery/Danita Delimont; 23 (UP RT), Jim Brandenburg/Minden Pictures; 23 (LO LE), Klein & Hubert/Nature Picture Library; 23 (LO RT), Ann & Steve Toon/Nature Picture Library; 24, Eric Baccega/Nature Picture Library

Printed in the United States of America
24/WOR/1